Favorite Fairy Tales

EMPEROR'S NEW CLOTHES

Retold by Rochelle Larkin   **Illustrated by Yvette Banek**

The Playmore/Waldman® is a registered trademark of Playmore Inc. Publishers
and Waldman Publishing Corp., New York, New York

The Playmore/Waldman Bug Logo® is a registered trademark of Playmore Inc. Publishers
and Waldman Publishing Corp., New York, New York

Once upon a time there lived an emperor who was only interested in one thing: beautiful new clothes for himself. He didn't worry about anything else.

All of the work of the country had to be done by other people. All the emperor wanted was to wear as many different outfits as he could each day, and to spend his time admiring himself in his hundreds of mirrors.

One day, two strangers appeared. They pretended to be special tailors, but they were really two bad men who were going to take advantage of the emperor's vanity.

"We have woven a very fine cloth," they said. "There is nothing quite like it anywhere in the world."

The emperor was delighted, but he tried not to show his interest too much. "What is so wonderful about this cloth?" he asked.

"This cloth is so remarkable that only the most remarkable people can see it," said the first man.

"If someone does not deserve his position, he will not be able to see the cloth at all," the other man went on.

The emperor knew at once he had to have a suit made from this cloth. Not only would it make splendid clothes for him, it would tell him if any of his ministers or other officials were undeserving of their jobs.

"Start at once," he ordered.

A house in the city was given over to the two men for the work. All day long they could be seen scurrying about, upstairs and down, acting as busy as if they really had been doing anything.

In spite of all this activity, the emperor was very impatient. He couldn't wait to see himself in the clothes that the two promised no one else in the whole world would have. He sent for his chief minister.

"Go to the two tailors," he commanded. "Report to me at once when I will be getting my new clothes."

"Yes, sire," said the minister, bowing and smiling his way out of the royal presence. But he wasn't really happy.

"Suppose," he thought as he went along, "suppose I'm not clever enough to see this cloth? What if I'm not fit for my high office? Whatever will I do then?"

The two men welcomed him. One pretended to hold a length of cloth. "Look, minister," he said, "isn't this the most beautiful color, the finest weave you've ever seen?"

The minister rubbed his eyes. He couldn't see any cloth at all.

"Yes, yes," the minister said. "It's the finest thing I've ever seen." But he knew he hadn't seen anything at all.

Back he went to the palace. "Oh majesty," he said, "it's the finest, the most beautiful, the most. . ."
He ran out of breath trying to describe what he hadn't seen.

The emperor was even more eager for his fine new clothes.
"But what," he thought, "if I can not see them? Am I really fit
to be emperor?"

The only person as concerned about the emperor's new clothes as the emperor himself was the dressing-servant. So the emperor sent him to see the cloth, while he himself tried to be satisfied with the clothes he already had.

But when the dressing-servant reported on the unequalled beauty of the clothes, the emperor lost all his patience.

"Give them more gold, give them more everything!" he ordered the treasurer. "Only get me those clothes!"

Excitement ran through the kingdom. People were full of curiosity about the fine new clothes. Each one worried about whether he or she would be able to see them.

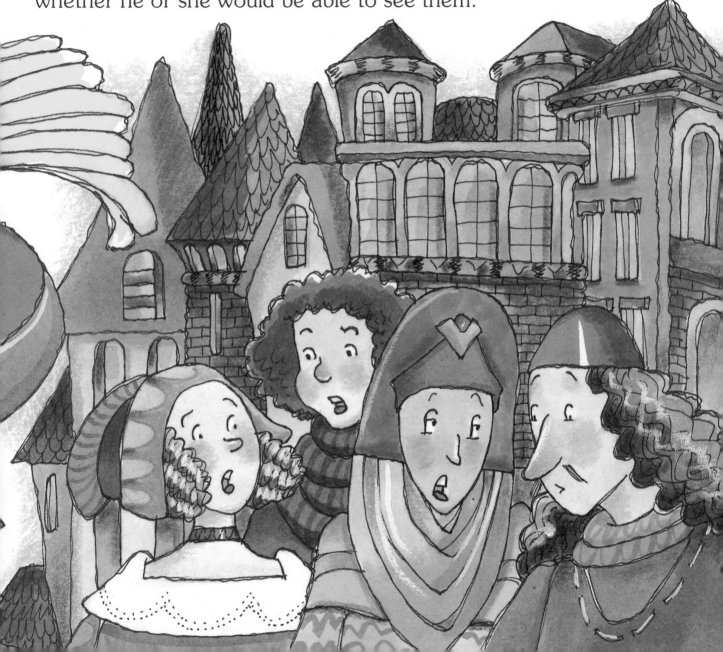

At last the great day came. The two tailors, who had been given as much gold as they could carry, announced that all was ready. The carriage to take them quickly out of the country was ready too, but they didn't announce that.

Up they strode to the palace, right into the emperor's vast
dressing-room, looking as proud and important as they could,
pretending to be carrying the precious clothes.

The emperor stood on a little platform, a mirror in his hand, mirrors all around him, still more mirrors held by all his servants, and all the ministers and members of the court gathered around him.

The two men fussed about, pretending to be fitting the clothes, making him turn this way and that.

The emperor peered at himself in the mirror, pretending he was wearing the finest clothes. But no one could see a single stitch.

"Perfect!" said one of the tailors.

"Perfect!" said the other. "Now your majesty must go out and show the rest of his country. Let us see if your subjects are fit for their jobs."

A grand parade was organized. The people all gathered. Everyone ooh'ed and aah'ed as the emperor strolled along.

"How beautiful! How beautiful!" all the people said to each other.

All except one little boy. "But the emperor has no clothes on!" he cried.

Everyone tried to quiet the little boy. But they all had to admit the truth, even the emperor, as he raced back to the palace.

As for the two strangers, they were already gone. No more was ever seen of them, or of the gold they had taken, than was ever seen of the cloth they had pretended to weave.